USBORNE
ANIMAL STORIES FOR BEDTIME

Retold by Susanna Davidson and Katie Daynes

Illustrated by Richard Johnson

CONTENTS

THE TOWN MOUSE
AND THE
COUNTRY MOUSE

A little furry mouse lived in a
burrow by a river. His nest
was soft with leaves, his cupboards
stuffed with berries.

One morning, the little mouse heard a rustling in the undergrowth.

"Surprise!" called a familiar voice. It was his big cousin from the town.

"I thought I'd pay you a visit," the Town Mouse said, "and get some country air."

"How lovely to see you," replied the Country Mouse. "I hope you like it here."

The Town Mouse looked at the towering trees and looming hills. "So, what shall we do?" he asked.

"Let's find some grass to make your bed and gather some nuts for dinner," said the Country Mouse. "Then I'll take you to the waterfall..."

The Town Mouse twitched his whiskers hesitantly. "Lead the way," he said, and scampered after his little cousin.

By sunset he was wet, tired and starving.

"Don't you have anything other than nuts and berries to eat?" he asked.

The Country Mouse offered him some seeds.

"Yuck," spluttered the Town Mouse. He stretched out in his bed. "This grass is too scratchy. I'd prefer newspaper."

The Country Mouse found him some moss.

"I suppose that's *slightly* softer..."

The next day, it just rained and rained and rained. The Country Mouse was happy weaving grass and making berry jelly, but his cousin was bored.

"There's nothing to *do*," he complained. "You must come and stay with me. There's never a dull moment where *I* live."

A shy smile crept beneath the Country Mouse's whiskers. "Why not?" he said.

The next day, they set off through the quiet woods and down a country lane. Gradually, buildings rose up on either side. People tramped up and down and cars roared back and forth.

It was evening before they reached the Town Mouse's home. The sky glowed orange with street lights and the noise from the road was deafening.

"Watch out for the bike!" cried the Town Mouse, as whirling wheels whizzed past them.

"It-it-it nearly hit me!" said the frightened Country Mouse.

"You're fine! Just follow me closely."

He climbed into a pipe,
crawled along a stinky tunnel,
and came out through a hole
into a large, tiled kitchen.

"Dinner time!"
announced the Town Mouse.

The Country Mouse let out a squeak of
delight. He'd never seen so much food. The
table was laden with cakes and the floor was
flecked with crumbs.

"Let's eat!" said the Town Mouse, grappling
his way up the tablecloth.

His wide-eyed cousin scrambled after him. "I
don't know where to start..." he murmured.

He was nibbling on a cake crumb when...

"Cat!" cried the Town Mouse. A large tabby cat had padded silently into the room and was crouching, ready to pounce.

"This way!" the Town Mouse shouted, racing the length of the table and making a daring leap for the mousehole under the kitchen sink.

His little cousin scurried after him, reached the edge of the table and froze.

It was a long way down.

MEOW! went the cat behind him, sending the terrified mouse over the edge. He landed with a bump and tumbled into the mousehole, missing the cat's outstretched claws by a whisker.

"What did I tell you?" said the Town Mouse, cheerfully. "Never a dull moment."

The Country Mouse stared in wonder at his cousin's clean, airy home.

Then he saw a large eye glinting through the entrance hole and a shiver ran down his tail. "How can you ever relax?" he whispered.

"Who wants to relax when there's an adventure around every corner?" replied the Town Mouse. He slid open a matchbox to reveal a golden nugget of cheese. "Here, have a bite."

"Thanks," said the Country Mouse, "but I'm not hungry anymore. I just want to go home."

"To your quiet little burrow?" asked the Town Mouse in surprise.

His cousin nodded. "I think I'd rather have berries and nuts in peace," he said, "than cheese and pie in fear."

The Town Mouse opened his mouth to reply, then shrugged and took a bite of cheese instead.

The next morning, he waved his cousin goodbye. "Come and visit any time!" he cried.

"You too!" replied the Country Mouse.

Do you think they ever did?

THE ELEPHANT'S NOSE

Long, long ago, the elephant had no
trunk – just a little nose, no bigger
than a sausage. She could jiggle it
and wiggle it and waggle it about,
but that was all.

And then along came the Elephant's Child. She was only a little elephant, but she was full of big questions.

"Aunt Ostrich," she said. "Why do your tail feathers grow just so?"

"Uncle Giraffe," she asked. "Why is your skin all spotty?"

"Great Aunt Hippopotamus, why are your eyes so red? Hairy Uncle Baboon, why do melons taste as they do?"

"Run along!" cried her uncles and aunts. "And STOP asking questions."

But the Elephant's Child wanted answers, and she wouldn't be satisfied till she got them.

One day, she asked a new question, one she'd never asked before. "What does a Crocodile have for dinner?"

And everyone said, "Hush!" in quivery, quavery voices.

"But I want to *know*," said the Elephant's Child. "I really do."

"No, you don't," said her uncles and aunts.

And that would have been that, if the Elephant's Child hadn't met the Kolokolo bird, who decided to help her.

"Go all the way to the great, green, greasy Limpopo River," he said. "That's where you'll find your answer."

So the Elephant's Child set out, with a little picnic of red bananas, purple sugarcane and seventeen greeny-juicy melons. She trudged all the way to the Limpopo River, then looked around for a Crocodile. Except, she realized, she had no idea what a Crocodile looked like. She had never seen one before. All she could see was a log.

The log opened one eye, and winked at her. (The log, you see, was actually a Crocodile.)

"Excuse me," said the Elephant's Child, very politely. "Have you seen a Crocodile in these parts?"

The Crocodile winked the other eye and lifted its tail out of the mud. "Come closer, little one. *I* am the Crocodile!"

"Oh!" said the Elephant's Child, coming closer, very breathless and excited. "Will you please tell me what you have for dinner?"

"Come closer, little one," said the Crocodile, "and I will whisper."

The Elephant's Child put her head close to the Crocodile's toothsome mouth and SNAP! The Crocodile caught her by her little nose. "I think," said the Crocodile, between his teeth, "that today, *you* will be my dinner!"

"*Led go!*" cried the Elephant's Child. "*You are hurdig be!*" And she sat back and pulled and pulled as hard as she could. As she did, her nose began to stretch.

The Crocodile floundered in the water, flailing around with his great tail, and *he* pulled and pulled as hard as *he* could.

The Elephant's Child's nose kept on stretching until it was so loooooooong!

She felt her feet slipping in the mud. "*This is too buch for me,*" she said. But at last, the Crocodile let go, landing back in the river with a PLOP that could be heard all the way along the Limpopo.

And SPLAT! The Elephant's Child fell back in the mud, her poor long nose dangling in front of her.

"Ow!" said the Elephant's Child. "It hurts."

So she wrapped her nose
up in cool banana leaves
and waited for it to shrink.
She waited *three* days, but
although it stopped hurting,
it didn't get any smaller.

At the end of the third day, a fly came and
rested on her shoulder and stung her.

Before she knew what she was doing,
the Elephant's Child lifted up her nose and
whacked the fly away.

"I couldn't have done that with my *old* nose,"
thought the Elephant's Child.

Next, she put out her nose, lifted up a
bundle of grass and stuffed it in her mouth. And
when she felt hot, she scooped up a schloop
of mud from the banks of the Limpopo and
slapped it on her head, where it made a cool

sloshy mud cap, all trickly behind her ears.

The Elephant's Child *loved* her new nose. So she went home to show it off.

"What have you done?" cried her family.

"I got a new nose from the Crocodile on the banks of the great, green, greasy Limpopo River," said the Elephant's Child. "I asked him what he had for dinner and he gave me this to keep."

Then all the other elephants set off one by one to get new noses from the Crocodile.

And that is why all the elephants you will ever see, and all the ones you won't, will have noses exactly like the Elephant's Child.

THE THREE LITTLE PIGS

Little pigs don't stay little forever.
There comes a time when
they must find homes
of their own...

"Make sure you build strong, safe houses," warned Mother Pig, as she waved goodbye to her three darling piglets.

"Of course, Mother," replied the first.

"Don't worry," said the second.

"We'll be fine," added the third.

And off they trotted, three not so little pigs, a curl in their tails and not a care in the world.

"Straw for sale!" called a farmer. "Fine and long. Golden yellow. Nature's best."

"Perfect," said the first pig.

He bought three big bundles and made himself a handsome straw hut.

"That was easy," he thought, as he waved goodbye to his brother and sister.

"Build strong, safe houses!" he called after
them, putting on their mother's voice.

The two pigs laughed and trotted
on into a forest.

"Sticks for sale!" called a
woodcutter. "Straight, brown
and strong."

"Ah ha," said the second
pig. "Sticks are better than
straw." She bought three big
bundles and made herself a
sturdy stick house. Then she waved goodbye to
her brother. "Make sure *you* build a strong, safe
house," she said, her piggy eyes twinkling.

On trotted the third pig to a factory by a
river. A sign above the door said: BRICKS FOR
SALE, so he bought three pallets of bricks and
a bucket of cement.

It was hard work carrying the heavy bricks and even harder building a brick house, but at last he had a strong, safe home of his own.

Little did the pigs know that a big bad wolf had been following their every move. Prowling the hedgerow, he watched the first pig trot into his handsome straw hut. The wolf licked his lips greedily and strolled up to the door.

"Little pig, little pig, let me in," he growled.

"Not by the hair of my chinny-chin-chin!" replied the pig in a panic.

"Then I'll huff and I'll puff and I'll *blow* your house in."

And he huffed and he puffed, and WHOOSH he blew the house in.

"Help!" squealed the pig, running as fast as his trotters could carry him to his sister's stick house. He only just made it before the wolf was rattling at the door.

"Little pigs, little pigs, let me in," he growled.

"Not by the hairs of our chinny-chin-chins!" replied the petrified pigs.

"Then I'll huff and I'll puff and I'll *blow* your house in."

And he huffed and he puffed...

And he huffed and he puffed...

And CRREEAK he blew the house in.

"Help!" squealed the little pigs, running to their brother's brick house. They felt the wolf's hot breath on their curly tails and quickly shut the door behind them.

"Little pigs, little pigs, let me in!" growled the big bad wolf.

"Not by the hairs of our chinny-chin-chins!"

"Then I'll huff and I'll puff and I'll *blow* your house in."

And he huffed and he puffed...

And he huffed and he puffed...

He huffed and puffed and huffed and puffed... But he just couldn't blow the house in.

"I'm coming to get you!" he yelled suddenly. In one leap he was on the roof. In two leaps he was sliding down the chimney...

He never managed a third leap. He had fallen SPLOSH into a bubbling cooking pot.

The little pigs quickly slammed on the lid, and that was the end of the big bad wolf.

THE LITTLE RED HEN

O nce upon a time, in a dusty, cobbled farmyard, a little red hen went peck, peck, peck.

A sleek tabby cat watched her sleepily from a wall, while a proud white goose stood preening her feathers, and a large greedy rat nibbled at a stale crumb.

All of a sudden, the little red hen raised her head. "Grains of wheat!" she clucked excitedly.

"So what?" sniffed the rat. "The farmer scatters them for you every day."

"But we could *plant* them," she announced.

The other animals looked at her as if she were crazy.

"Come on," clucked the hen. "Who's going to help me?"

"Not I," said the rat.

"Not I," said the goose.

"Not I," said the cat.

The hen looked
disappointed.
"Then I shall do
it all by myself,"
she replied. And
she did.

Grain by grain, the hen
carried the wheat in her beak to the edge of
a field. She pecked little holes in the lumpy
brown earth, gently dropped the grains in
and scraped some soil over the top. Then she
walked back to the farmyard.

"Where is your wheat now?" asked the cat,
licking his paws.

"Growing," replied the hen.

And it was. First, bright green shoots popped
their heads out of the soil, then they grew taller,
darker, stronger.

Finally, under the gaze of the summer sun, the wheat plants turned from green to gold.

"It's ready!" cried the hen, fluffing her feathers in delight. "Who will help me to cut it down?"

"Not I," squeaked the rat.

"Not I," honked the goose.

"Not I," purred the cat.

"Then I shall do it all by myself," said the hen. And she did.

The cat, the goose and the rat watched idly from a distance as, one by one, the hen snipped the stalks with her beak. She looked proudly at the pile of golden wheat, then turned to the other animals.

"Now tell me," she clucked, making the cat jump. "Who's going to help me grind this lovely wheat into flour?"

"Not I," huffed the cat.

"Not I," echoed the goose.

"Not I," declared the rat.

"Then I shall do it all by myself," said the hen. And she did.

The others hardly looked up as she walked to and from the mill, carrying as much wheat as her beak could hold. With all her might, she turned the heavy millstone and ground the grains until she had a sack of flour.

"Who will help me make the flour into bread?" she asked, dragging the bag to the farmhouse kitchen.

"Not I," sighed the goose.

"Not I," yawned the cat.

"Not I," groaned the rat.

"Then I shall do that all by myself as well," she puffed.

And she did. She made the flour into a soft, stretchy dough. Before long, wafts of baking bread reached the animals in the farmyard. They rushed to the kitchen window and the goose eagerly tapped her beak on the glass.

The little red hen looked up, amused. "Who will help me eat this bread?" she asked.

"Me!" cried the cat.

"Me!" cried the goose.

"Me!" cried the rat.

"Oh no you won't," said the little red hen, turning back to her warm, crusty loaf. "I had to make this bread all by myself, so I shall eat it *all by myself*."

And she did.

THE BiLLY GOATS GRUFF

Once upon a time there were three Billy Goats, and the name of all three was Gruff.

"I'm hungry," said big Billy Goat Gruff one day.
"Me too," said middle-sized Billy Goat Gruff.
"Me three," said little Billy Goat Gruff.

Big Billy Goat Gruff looked around, at the
bare brown ground. "We need to find more
grass," he announced in his great gruff voice.
"We'll have to cross the Rushing River, to reach
the green fields beyond."

Little Billy Goat Gruff climbed
on some rocks to see. There,
beyond the Rushing River, were
meadows thick with sweet, juicy
grass. He was so excited by the
thought of all that delicious grass
in his tummy, he decided to leave
right away. He jumped down
from the rocks and dashed
along the path to the bridge.

42

Clippety-clop, clippety-clop went his hooves
all along the path, then
TRIP-TRAP, TRIP-TRAP,

TRIP-TRAP
as he trotted across the bridge.

Little Billy Goat Gruff was so busy gazing at
the grass, that he never noticed the big, green
hairy hands gripping the sides of the bridge.

"Who's that tripping over MY bridge?" roared
a terrible, rumbling voice.

Little Billy Goat Gruff stopped and stared at the green hairy hands. He gulped. "It is only I," he said, in a small squeaky voice, "a tiny little billy goat going to the grassy fields..."

"I'm coming to gobble you up!" roared the voice, and a huge and warty troll heaved himself onto the bridge.

"Oh no! Don't eat me," cried the little billy goat. "Why don't you wait for middle-sized Billy Goat Gruff? He's much bigger and fatter than me."

"Humph," said the troll. "You are tiny. No more than a snack really. Be off with you!"

Little Billy Goat Gruff scampered off the bridge in a flash.

The troll hid under his bridge, and waited...

Soon, middle-sized Billy Goat Gruff came to the river. His hooves went

TRIP-TRAP, TRIP-TRAP, TRIP-TRAP

as he trotted across the bridge.

"Who's that tripping over MY bridge?" roared the troll.

"It's only me," said middle-sized Billy Goat Gruff, in his not-so-squeaky voice. "I'm going to the grassy fields to make myself round and fat."

"I'm coming to gobble you up!" said the troll, and he leaped onto the bridge.

Middle-sized Billy Goat Gruff looked at the troll and started to quiver and quake.

"Oh no!" he cried. "Why don't you wait until big Billy Goat Gruff comes? He's much bigger and fatter than me."

"Humph!" said the troll, crouching back under the bridge. "I've waited this long, I suppose I can wait a little longer. But this billy goat had better be *really* fat and *really* juicy!"

"Oh yes," said middle-sized Billy Goat Gruff.

"Be off with you, then," said the troll, and middle-sized Billy Goat Gruff ran.

The troll licked his lips and waited...

Soon there was a

TRIP-TRAP, TRIP-TRAP, TRIP-TRAP

much louder than before.

The whole bridge creaked and groaned under big Billy Goat Gruff's great weight.

The troll smiled. "This is going to be a very tasty meal," he thought.

"Who's that tramping over MY bridge?" he roared, as he leaped onto the bridge.

"It is I! Big Billy Goat Gruff!" said the billy goat, in his great gruff voice.

"I'm going to gobble you up!" cried the troll.

"Oh no you're not," retorted Big Billy Goat Gruff. He stamped his hooves and reared up.

Then he flew at the troll, horns lowered, and with a mighty BAM, tossed him into the water.

The troll landed with an enormous SPLASH! He grunted and groaned and waved his fists furiously. But there was nothing he could do. He was swept down the rushing river.

As for the billy goats, they spent the rest of their days in the grassy meadows, growing round and fat and happy. The huge and warty troll was never seen again.

And so...

Snip, snap, snout,
this tale's told out.

MOUSE DEER AND THE CROCODILE

Mouse Deer was oh so thirsty
as he ran down to the river
to drink. But could he? Or was
Crocodile lurking there?

He listened to the sounds of the
jungle – the chattering monkeys, the
croaking frogs. But no sound came from
the river. "Perhaps it's safe..." thought
Mouse Deer, creeping closer to the water on his
tiny pointy hooves.

Then he remembered how still and silent
Crocodile could be. "I'll just make sure," Mouse
Deer decided...

He cleared his throat. "I wonder if the
water's warm," he said, as loudly as he could.
He picked up a long stick and dipped the tip
into the water.

CHOMP! Crocodile's jaws grabbed hold of
the stick and yanked it.

"Hee hee!" laughed Mouse Deer. "Don't you know a stick from a leg, Mr. Crocodile?"

Crocodile spat out the stick. His cold eyes stared at Mouse Deer. "I'll get you next time," he snapped.

Mouse Deer put his nose in the air and danced away, singing,

I'm a Mouse Deer,
Clever as can be,
Ha! Mr. Crocodile,
You can't catch me!

Mouse Deer skipped through the forest, nibbling on leaves and splashing in puddles, but soon he longed to drink again from the wide, wide river. Was Crocodile still there?

Mouse Deer looked left, Mouse Deer looked right. Nothing was in the river, he decided. Just an old log, floating on the surface. At last, he could drink! Then Mouse Deer remembered – Crocodile looked like a log when he floated.

"I'll just make sure..." he decided.

Mouse Deer cleared his throat. "If that log is really Crocodile, it won't talk. But if it's only a log, it will tell me."

A deep, gravelly voice, like the sound of grinding stones, replied, "I'm only a log."

Mouse Deer laughed. "I've tricked you twice now, Mr. Crocodile. Do you really think a log can talk?" And he skipped away, singing his teasing song,

> *I'm a Mouse Deer,*
> *Clever as can be,*
> *Ha! Mr. Crocodile,*
> *You can't catch me!*

Crocodile was furious. "I won't let him trick me again," he swore. And he did what crocodiles do best – he waited.

It wasn't long before Mouse Deer came back. He wasn't thirsty now, but he was yearning to eat the tasty, juicy, succulent fruit on the other side of the river.

The trouble was, he'd be chomped by Crocodile if he tried to swim across. Unless...

"Oh Mr. Crocodile!" Mouse Deer called out.

Crocodile gave a toothy grin.

"Good afternoon, Mouse Deer," he said. "Have you come to be eaten at last? You'd make a wonderful snack."

Mouse Deer shook his head. "I have orders from the King," he announced.

"From the King?" asked Crocodile.

"Oh yes," said Mouse Deer. "He always gives his most important orders to me."

"And what exactly does the King want?"

"He wants me to count all crocodiles. Today! You must line up from this side of the river to the other."

"Well if it's for the King," said Crocodile. "Of course I'll do it."

He called to his friends and family and
they lined up neatly across the river, just like a
floating bridge.

"Stay as still as you can," ordered Mouse
Deer. "We mustn't get this wrong for the King."

Mouse Deer jumped onto Crocodile's back.
"One!" he called.

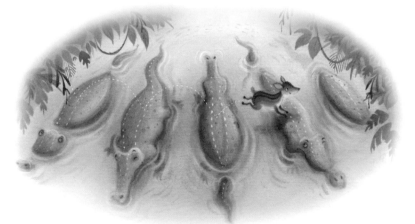

He jumped onto the next crocodile. "Two!"
And the next. "Three!"

Mouse Deer kept jumping until he jumped
all the way to the other side of the river.

"How many are there?" asked Crocodile.

"Just enough to get me across," said Mouse Deer with a smile. "I've tricked you again, Mr. Crocodile!" And he skipped away to eat the juicy fruits, singing,

I'm a Mouse Deer,
Clever as can be,
Ha! Mr. Crocodile,
You'll never catch me!

CHICKEN LICKEN

There was once a little chicken
with a wild imagination.
His name was Chicken Licken
and he lived on a farm.

While the other farm animals felt happy and safe, Chicken Licken saw danger at every turn. He'd see a shadow and think it was a three-eyed monster, or hear the tractor's engine and think it was a fire-breathing dragon.

One day, Chicken Licken was standing nervously near a towering oak tree, wondering if it was actually a fearsome ogre. Suddenly an acorn fell from the tree and hit him.

BONK!

"Ouch!" yelped Chicken Licken, looking up. He didn't see the acorn. Instead, he saw the sky above.

"The sky is falling!" he cried in a panic. "I must tell the King." And he raced off.

"Out of my way!" he called as he passed Henny Penny by the hen house.

"Whatever's the matter?" clucked the hen.

"The sky is falling!" cried Chicken Licken.

"Oh no," she gasped. "What shall we do?"

"I'm going to tell the King," announced Chicken Licken.

"Then I'll come too," Henny Penny replied.

They raced on together and met Cocky Locky, the rooster.

"What's going on?" he asked.

"The sky is falling!" cried Chicken Licken. "We're going to tell the King."

"Then I'll come too," Cocky Locky replied.

They rushed on past the duck pond.

"What's up?" quacked Ducky Lucky.

"The sky is falling!" cried Chicken Licken. "We're going to tell the King."

"Then I'll come too," Ducky Lucky replied.

On they sped, past the old barn where Goosey Loosey sat on her nest.

"What's happening?" she called out.

"The sky is falling!" cried Chicken Licken. "We're going to tell the King."

"Then I'll come too," Goosey Loosey replied.

They ran into the field where Turkey Lurkey was pecking for worms.

"What's all the fuss?" he asked.

"The sky is falling!" cried Chicken Licken. "We're going to tell the King."

"Then I'll come too," Turkey Lurkey replied.

And on they ran, deep into the royal forest: Chicken Licken, Henny Penny, Cocky Locky, Ducky Lucky, Goosey Loosey and Turkey Lurkey.

Watching them, from the shadow of an oak tree, was cunning Foxy Loxy.

"Whatever's the matter?" he asked.

"The sky is falling!" cried Chicken Licken. "We're going to the palace to warn the King," added Turkey Lurkey. "Is that right?" asked Foxy Loxy. "Then I'll show you a shortcut."

He pointed down a tunnel and the animals rushed inside. Oh no – a dead end! And there was Foxy Loxy, baring his teeth at the entrance.

"This isn't the way to the palace..." said Henny Penny.

"No," snarled Foxy Loxy. "This is where I keep my DINNER!"

Just then, the terrified animals saw an acorn fall from the tree and hit Foxy Loxy BONK on his head.

"Ouch!" said Foxy Loxy. He didn't see the acorn. Instead, he looked up in horror. "The sky really is falling," he cried, and ran off into the forest.

The other animals sighed with relief, then looked sternly at Chicken Licken.

"Do you still think we need to warn the King?" asked Goosey Loosey.

"Um, no," said Chicken Licken. "Sorry about that."

And they chased him all the way home.

THE MUSICIANS OF BREMEN

Once upon a time, a cruel farmer wanted to get rid of his tired old donkey. "I'll run away," decided the donkey, "and become a musician."

So he set off down the road to the city of Bremen, to join the town band. On his way he met a hunting dog, collapsed in a sorry heap. "What's the matter?" asked the donkey.

"I've run away from my master," sighed the dog. "He wanted to shoot me because I'm too old to hunt. So I escaped, but now I have nowhere to go."

"Why not come to Bremen with me?" the donkey suggested. "I'm going to be a musician. You can play the drums while I play the piano."

"What a good idea!" said the dog.

And the pair walked on, thinking up tunes. They hadn't gone far when they met a bedraggled cat.

"What's the matter?" asked the donkey.

"My mistress tried to drown me," spat the cat, "because I've grown too old to chase mice. All I want is a quiet life by the kitchen stove, but she won't have it."

"Then come with us!" said the dog.

"We're going to be musicians in Bremen," explained the donkey. "I'm going to play the piano, Dog is going to play drums and I bet you'd make an excellent violinist."

The cat thought this was a brilliant plan, and padded along beside them.

It was getting dark as they neared a farm. Perched on the barn roof was a rooster, crowing at the top of his voice.

COCK-A-DOODLE-DOOOOOOOOOO!

"Why are you crowing now?" asked the donkey. "It's night-time, not morning."

"I'm going to be roasted for dinner tomorrow," sobbed the rooster. "Tonight is my last night."

"It doesn't have to be," said the donkey. "Run away with us. We're going to be musicians in Bremen."

"You can be our singer," said the cat.

"Lead the way!" said the rooster, and the four animals set off together.

Soon they reached a shadowy forest.

"Let's stay here tonight," said the donkey.

"I'm starving," moaned the dog.

"I'm freezing," shivered the cat.

The rooster flew to the top branch of a tree. "Hang on," he called, "I can see a light up ahead. Maybe someone lives there?"

The animals followed the light and found a curious house among the trees.

The donkey crept closer and peered in at the window.

"I see a table of food!" he said in excitement. "And a band of robbers," he added in dismay.

"I have an idea..." whispered the cat.

They huddled closer to hear her plan.
Then the dog climbed on the donkey, the cat
climbed on the dog, the rooster climbed on the
cat and, when the cat said, "Now!" they all burst
into song.

The robbers were so startled by the
cacophony, they jumped up and raced out of the
door without looking back.

The animals couldn't believe their luck.
There was roast beef for the dog, fresh bread for
the rooster, baked fish for the cat and a whole
chocolate cake for the donkey. Happy and full
at last, the animals blew out the candles and lay
down to sleep.

But the robbers hadn't gone far. They were
hiding in the trees, waiting for a chance to
come back.

As the house went quiet and dark, the chief robber turned to the littlest member of the gang.

"Go and see who's stolen our hideout," he ordered gruffly.

All was still as the little robber tiptoed into the dark kitchen. He saw the cat's eyes gleaming and thought they were burning coals in a fireplace. "Just what I need," he murmured. He poked his candle at the coals, hoping to light it.

"AIIIEEEEK!" squealed the cat, leaping up and scratching the intruder.

Terrified, the robber ran to the back door and tripped over the dog, who snapped at him.

"Ouch!"

He hobbled into the yard where he was bucked by the donkey.

"Owwwww!"

This woke the rooster, who gave a deafening

COCK-A-DOODLE-DOO from the rooftop.

Scared out of his mind, the robber shot back into the forest.

"Quick!" he shouted to the other robbers. "We must get out of here. I've just been scratched by a witch, stabbed on the leg, hit with a club, and now an evil voice is yelling, 'Catch that rascal do!'"

The band of robbers turned and fled, and never returned to the house in the forest.

As for the animals, they never did become musicians. They didn't even make it to Bremen. They liked their new home so much, they decided to stay – and there they lived happily, for the rest of their lives.

THE HARE AND THE TORTOISE

I t was March, and Hare had gone
mad. He was springing through the
air like a wild thing, bashing down
daffodils and leaping over grassy hills.

The other animals watched in wonder.

"Bonkers," said the mole.

"Bananas," chattered the caterpillars.

"A crazy crazed crazy thing," laughed the lop-eared rabbits.

"Not I! Not I!" said Hare, bounding up to them, boxing the air with his fists. "It's Spring! Can't you feel it? I'm bounding with energy. Bursting with life."

Tortoise shook his head. "Here we go again," he muttered. "He's the same every year – full of talk, and it gets him nowhere."

"Nonsense," snapped Hare. "I'm in my prime. I could do anything. Run to the moon and back before you could creep across this field."

"I think not," said Tortoise. "You're like a bag of hot air. All puff, no substance."

"Is that a challenge?" cried Hare.

"If you want it to be," Tortoise sighed.

"Then a race it shall be!" Hare jumped joyously in the air. "First to the oak tree and back. *On your marks, get set, GO!*"

And he was off, bursting forward like a furry rocket. Tortoise rolled his eyes and plodded after him.

"Poor old Tortoise," said Mole. "He'll never win."

Hare made it to the oak tree in no time. He turned back and saw Tortoise, a speck in the distance, going PLOD, PLOD, PLOD...

"Ha!" laughed Hare. "No contest there. I might as well lie down and rest."

He curled up under the oak tree and promptly fell fast asleep.

PLOD, PLOD, PLOD went Tortoise, past the oak tree and back across the field. He moved very slowly, but he never stopped.

As the sun began to set, he neared the finish line. "Come on, Tortoise!" cheered the other animals.

Their voices carried on the wind and Hare woke with a start. "What's this? What's this?" he said, looking around. Then he spotted Tortoise. "Noooo!" he wailed. Using every muscle he possessed, he zipped across the field, tearing towards the finish line like the wind.

But he was too late. Tortoise was already there. "Just as I remarked," said Tortoise. "You're all talk. Slow and steady wins the race, you see."

THE UGLY DUCKLING

Crack! Crack! Peep, peep, peep,
peep! One by one, Mother
Duck's eggs were bursting open.
One... two... three... four fluffy little
ducklings came tumbling out.

"Aren't you perfect!" clucked Mother Duck. "Just one more to go." She turned and looked impatiently at the last egg. It was huge, much larger than the others, and rather dull and mottled. "Hmm," said Mother Duck. "Well, I suppose I'd better wait for you too."

As the sun was going down, the last egg finally began to break. Out crept the duckling. "Oh dear!" gasped Mother Duck. The duckling was very large, and very ugly.

The other ducks came over to see.

"Looks like a turkey chick to me," said an old duck. "Take it for a swim and see if it sinks."

So early the next morning, Mother Duck waddled down to the river, her four little fluffy ducklings following on behind. The Ugly Duckling came last, looking forlorn, his head bent low. "Turkey chick! Turkey chick!" chanted his brothers and sisters.

When they reached the water, Mother Duck watched as they all jumped in. Splish! Splosh! Splish! Splosh! SPLASH! Mother Duck held her breath, but all five bobbed back up again. "So he's not a turkey chick," thought Mother Duck. "Just a *very* ugly duckling."

Everyone else thought so too. The turkey in the farmyard gobbled at him. The farm girl tried to shoo him away. The farm dog barked; the farm cat hissed.

His brothers and sisters just laughed at him.
"You're the ugliest duckling we've *ever* seen!"
"I'll fly away," decided the Ugly Duckling.
"I'll fly away and never come
back." He flapped his little
wings and flew over the
farmyard fence. The gusty
wind swept him on and
on. He soared over
rivers and lakes until,
at last, exhausted, he
flopped down on a wild
and boggy moor.

"I'm all alone,"
sniffed the Ugly
Duckling. "But at least
there's no one to laugh at
me here."

And he tucked his head under his wing.

BANG! BANG! Shots tore through the air. The Ugly Duckling looked up and squawked as two wild ducks fell down beside him. A great hunt was going on. The moors were suddenly alive with men, stalking along with guns, hunting dogs bounding beside them.

The Ugly Duckling crouched low among the grasses but a terrible dog had smelled him. He thrust his great black nose at the duckling, sniffed... and went on. "I am so ugly even a dog won't eat me," thought the Ugly Duckling.

On shaking wings, the Ugly Duckling flew on once more, until he came to a large lake. It was empty and glassy, silent and still.

"I'll live here," decided the Ugly Duckling.

He passed a lonely summer, watching and waiting as the leaves turned to orange and gold. As winter approached, the wind caught the leaves as they fell, and danced them on the frosty air.

One evening, just as the sun was setting, a flock of beautiful birds flew out of the bushes. The duckling had never seen anything like them before. They were swans, with long and graceful necks and glorious white wings, spread out across the sky.

The Ugly Duckling stretched out his neck towards them and uttered a cry so strange that it frightened him.

Then winter came. The ice on the lake froze so fast he was nearly trapped. The Ugly Duckling dragged himself out and collapsed on the newly fallen snow.

"I don't want to be alone," he thought. He watched the swirling snowflakes in the misty sky, remembering the beautiful birds.

The winter seemed to last forever, until one morning, the Ugly Duckling woke to feel the warm sun on his feathers. He heard the lark singing. Spring had come at last!

He flapped his wings and they felt sure and strong. He plunged into the lake, just as three swans came sailing by. The Ugly Duckling waited for them to laugh at him. He bowed his head in shame. But there... what was that in the water. Was it really his own reflection? The Ugly Duckling looked and looked again. It really was! He was a swan!

The other swans swam around him, wings outstretched in greeting. They rubbed his neck. They stroked his feathers. The Ugly Duckling was filled with joy.

"If only I'd known," he thought, "if only I'd guessed, when I was an Ugly Duckling, that one day I'd be as happy as this."

About the Stories

People all over the world have always enjoyed hearing stories about animals and imagining their adventures.

Over two thousand years ago, a Greek man named Aesop made up lots of animal fables. Each fable had a moral, or a lesson at the end. The Country Mouse learns that a 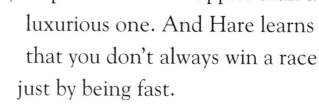 quiet, simple life can be happier than a luxurious one. And Hare learns that you don't always win a race just by being fast.

Many traditional tales, such as *The Three Little Pigs* and *Mouse Deer and the Crocodile*, have been passed down through the generations from our grandparents' grandparents. We don't know who first made them up, but we like the stories so much that we keep on telling them.

Two brothers in Germany, Jacob and Wilhelm Grimm, were famous for their collection of folk tales, first published in 1812. That's where our version of *The Musicians of Bremen* comes from, although it had probably been told for many years before then.

A decade later in Denmark, Hans Christian Andersen was writing his own stories, including *The Ugly Duckling*. He wrote adult books too, but he's best known for his spellbinding fairy tales.

Rudyard Kipling wrote a wonderful book, published in 1902, called the *Just So Stories*. It is full of amusing, inventive tales of how elephants and other animals became the way they are.

If you enjoy these stories and share them with others, who knows? People may still be telling them hundreds of years from now.

Edited by Lesley Sims

Designed by Caroline Spatz

First published in 2013 by Usborne Publishing Ltd., Usborne House,
83-85 Saffron Hill, London EC1N 8RT, England. www.usborne.com
Copyright © 2013 Usborne Publishing Ltd.